For Amy and Mia
- S. C.

Follow your heart, and look after those close to you.
- C. P.

tiger tales
5 River Road, Suite 128, Wilton, CT 06897
Published in the United States 2017
Originally published in Great Britain 2017
by Little Tiger Press
Text by Suzanne Chiew
Text copyright © 2017 Little Tiger Press
Illustrations copyright © 2017 Caroline Pedler
ISBN-13: 978-1-68010-040-2
ISBN-10: 1-68010-040-8
Printed in China
LTP/1800/1648/0916
10 9 8 7 6 5 4 3 2 1

For more insight and activities, visit us at www.tigertalesbooks.com

That's What Friends Are For

by Suzanne Chiew • Illustrated by Caroline Pedler

tiger tales

"What a glorious day!" beamed Badger
as he played happily in the summer sun.
"I haven't seen a cloud in weeks," Hedgehog
called from his sunflower patch.
And the baby bunnies sang, "Hooray for summer!"
as they splashed in their pool.

The next day, Badger was fixing
Rabbit's umbrella when Mouse
rushed up in a panic.
"Badger!" she cried. "Come quickly!
The stream has run out of water!"
"Run out of water?" exclaimed
Badger. "Let's go see!"

Rabbit and Hedgehog were running down to the stream, too. "Have you heard?" they cried frantically. "There's no water!" "Impossible!" chirped Bird, swooping down. "Whoever heard of such a thing?"

But at the stream, all they found was a teeny, tiny trickle—just enough to fill Badger's cup.

"Maybe there's more in the pond," suggested Bird, and she flew off to find out.

"This won't last long," said Badger. "We'd better find a way to collect the rest of the water."

Back home, Badger quickly built a sturdy barrel.
"We have an entire pot full of water," the bunnies
called as they ran up to Badger.
"And my teapot's full," added Rabbit.

But when they poured in everyone's water, the barrel wasn't even half full.

"How will I water my flowers?" exclaimed Hedgehog.

"How will we fill our pool?" wailed the baby bunnies.

"How will I do my laundry?" squeaked Mouse.

"Wait a minute," Badger said. "If there's no water left, what will we drink?"

As the summer sun's rays grew stronger, the friends fell silent.

"Maybe Bird will find water," said Hedgehog hopefully.

But Bird had terrible news.
"The pond is dry!" she twittered.
"The frogs have lost their home!"

"That's awful!" everyone
exclaimed. "What can we do?"

"We must share our water with the frogs," replied Badger.
  Being careful not to waste one drop, the friends poured some into Badger's wheelbarrow and headed for the pond.

They arrived just in time.

"We're so happy to see you!" croaked the frogs.

Badger picked them up and helped them into the wheelbarrow.

"Oh, thank you!" they ribbited,
splashing gratefully.
"Maybe we'll find more water
upstream," suggested Bird.
"Good idea!" beamed Badger.
"Let's go check."

But the journey uphill was steep, long, and very hot.

"I can't walk anymore," sighed Hedgehog.

"We're thirsty!" wailed the baby bunnies.

"We can't give up," said Badger. "I bet there's water just ahead."

The friends struggled along the path until around the bend, they saw . . .

. . . WATER!
A cool mountain pool sparkled in the sun.
"Jump in!" yelled the bunnies.

"I think these boulders have moved," said Badger. "They are stopping the water from flowing downstream."

"But they're too big for us to move out of the way," chirped Bird.

"Maybe not," said Badger. "I have an idea!"

Badger found a branch
to use as a lever.

He wedged one end under
the biggest rock and pushed
down hard on the other end.
But the boulder didn't budge.

"We'll help!" called the rabbits, and everyone rushed up.
"It's no good," twittered Bird. "It just won't move."
"Wait for us!" yelled the frogs. And just as the
smallest frog leapt onto the lever, the boulder
wobbled and started to roll!

WHOOSH went the water as it flowed
down the hill.
"HOORAY!" everyone cheered.

Soon the stream was flowing again, and then it finally started to rain.

"Your rain barrels work perfectly!" squeaked Mouse as raindrops dripped down into the barrels. "Now we can save water on rainy days."

"Hooray!" exclaimed the baby bunnies.

And everyone cheered, "Hooray for our clever friend Badger!"